# Jade
## the Disco
## Fairy

by Daisy Meadows

ORCHARD

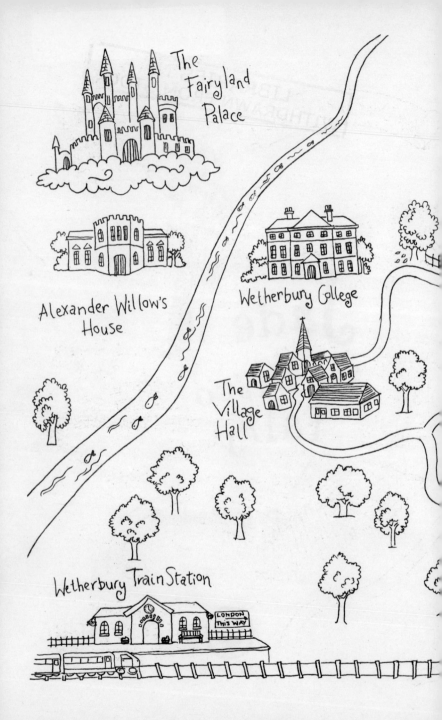

The Fairyland Palace

Alexander Willow's House

Wetherbury College

The Village Hall

Wetherbury Train Station

LONDON THIS WAY

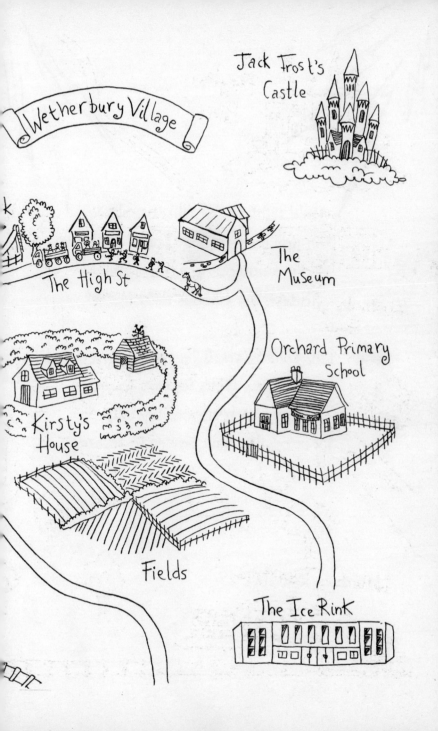

Hold tight to the ribbons, please.

You goblins now may feel a breeze.

I'm summoning a hurricane

To take the ribbons away again.


But, goblins, you'll be swept up too,

For I have work for you to do.

Guard each ribbon carefully,

By using this new power to freeze.

# Contents

# Girls Go Dancing

"Strike!" cheered Kirsty Tate, as Rachel's ball sent all ten pins flying at the end of the bowling lane.

"Hurrah!" Rachel cried in delight.

"That's your third strike of the game!" Kirsty's dad said, smiling. "Well done, Rachel."

"And it looks like you won the game,

too!" Mrs Tate added, gazing up at the electronic scoreboard in front of her.

The girls went to see. Sure enough, flashing green letters spelled out 'RACHEL WINS' on the screen.

"Yay!" Rachel said. "I'm having the best holiday ever – and it's only just begun!"

She and Kirsty grinned at each other.

Rachel was staying with Kirsty's family for the autumn half-term holiday, and the two girls always had very exciting adventures whenever they were together. *Fairy* adventures! This time was no different. Only yesterday, they'd met the seven Dance Fairies, who'd asked for their help. The girls had said yes straightaway. They loved helping the fairies!

"Well, girls," Mr Tate said as the scoreboard flashed 'GAME OVER'. "It's time to take off your bowling shoes, and put on your dancing shoes. It's the school disco this evening, remember?"

"I can't wait," Kirsty said eagerly. "Rachel and I love dancing, don't we?"

Rachel nodded, knowing Kirsty was thinking about the Dance Fairies. "Definitely," she replied. "Come on, let's go!"

Once they were back at the Tates' house, the girls got changed for the disco in Kirsty's bedroom. Rachel was wearing a pretty purple party dress, and Kirsty picked out a pink sparkly top and a pair of black trousers.

"I can't wait to see all your friends again," Rachel said, brushing her hair in front of the mirror.

"I really enjoyed meeting them at your birthday party. It'll be great to dance with them tonight."

Kirsty went over to check that her door was closed properly. "We might even get to see another of the Dance Fairies too!"

she added in a low voice.

"I hope so," Rachel said eagerly. Yesterday, she and Kirsty had met all seven Dance Fairies and been magically whisked away to Fairyland, where they'd learned that the Dance Fairies' magical ribbons had been stolen by the bad fairy, Jack Frost.

The fairies had explained that the magic ribbons made sure that dancing went smoothly and was fun, for everyone in Fairyland as well as in the human world. Jack Frost had stolen the ribbons because he wanted his goblins to be able to dance well at a party he was throwing.

Rachel and Kirsty, together with the Dance Fairies and the Fairy King and Queen, had gone to Jack Frost's ice castle to try and get the ribbons back.

But, when he saw them coming, sneaky Jack Frost had sent all the ribbons into the human world, along with a goblin to guard each one.

14

Yesterday, the girls had helped Bethany the Ballet Fairy find the goblin with her Ballet Ribbon, and they'd got the ribbon safely back, but they'd been shocked to discover that Jack Frost had given his goblin servants a new magical power. While they had the ribbons, the goblins could freeze anything they wanted with their master's icy magic!

Kirsty picked up a hair-clip and began fastening it in her hair. Then she stopped and looked at Rachel with a worried expression. "I've just had a thought," she said. "What if the school disco is ruined because the Disco Ribbon is still missing?"

Rachel bit her lip. "I hope it's not," she said. "It would be awful if the school dance was spoilt. We'll have to look out for the goblin, and hope that we can get the magic ribbon back to Jade the Disco Fairy before anything goes wrong."

Kirsty nodded. "I don't like the thought of meeting another goblin who can freeze us," she shivered, "but we've got to try and save the disco!"

## Groovy Goblin

"See you later, girls," Mrs Tate said,
as she dropped Kirsty and Rachel
off at the school hall that evening.
"Have fun!"

"Bye Mum, we will," Kirsty replied,
waving. She and Rachel walked
towards the doors. They could hear
music pounding as they approached

and exchanged hopeful looks.

"The disco seems to be going all right so far," Rachel said optimistically. "I mean, the music's playing, so it hasn't been cancelled or anything..."

Kirsty pushed open the doors. "Oh, and look!" she cried happily, "The hall is never usually this pretty!"

Rachel and Kirsty

gazed around the large school hall. Balloons and streamers were pinned in the top corners of the room and coloured lights flashed on the dance floor. Above their heads, sparkling glitter balls hung from the ceiling, sending tiny colourful reflections spinning all around the room. "Wow!" said Rachel.

"It looks great, but no one is dancing."
The girls looked at the empty dance
floor. There were clusters of girls and
boys all around
the room,
but nobody
was actually
dancing to
the music.
"Maybe it's
a good thing,"
Kirsty said in a low
voice. "While the Disco Ribbon isn't on
Jade's wand, everyone's dancing would
probably be really bad anyway."

Rachel was just about to agree when
the song changed and two adults took to
the dance floor, with rather self-conscious
smiles on their faces.

Kirsty's eyes widened. "It's Mr Collins and Mrs Adams!" she said.

"It looks like they're trying to get the disco started," Rachel added, watching as the teachers began to dance. Mr Collins started shaking his hips to the music, but somehow this caused his legs to go in opposite directions and he slipped on the floor and went flying into Mrs Adams. Mrs Adams wobbled as he crashed into her, and her arms flailed as she tried to keep her balance.

Kirsty looked at Rachel. "Oh, no," she said. "I was afraid this would happen!"

Rachel nodded. "We really need the Disco Ribbon!"

People around the room were giggling because the two teachers seemed to be getting worse by the second. Mrs Adams trod on Mr Collins' toes, then he knocked her glasses off as he attempted to do a groovy finger-pointing movement!

"They are *so* bad," a girl standing near Kirsty and Rachel giggled to her friends. "I can't believe they're such awful dancers!"

"Come on, we can't be any worse than them," one of her friends replied. "Let's go and show them how it's done!"

The group of girls edged onto the dance floor and started dancing, keeping a safe distance from the floundering teachers. Then another few girls joined them, followed by some boys. It seemed that the teachers' awful dancing had given everyone else a bit of confidence. In just a few minutes, the empty dance floor was packed.

"Shall we dance too?" Rachel asked, turning to Kirsty.

But Kirsty was staring at the dancers,

looking alarmed. "It's getting a bit dangerous out there, if you ask me!" she replied. "Look!" Rachel turned back to see that it wasn't just the teachers who were dancing badly now. *Nobody* seemed able to dance well at all! As Rachel watched in horror, she saw one girl lose

her balance and crash into her friend.
Then, on the other side of the room,
she saw a boy fall over, dragging
a couple of mates down with him.

"I've never seen such awful dancing,"
Rachel whispered to Kirsty in dismay.
"Someone's going to get hurt in
a minute!"

Kirsty nodded. "We really must find the ribbon," she whispered back, "before this turns into a disaster! Come on, let's start looking."

Rachel scanned the room, wondering where they should begin their search, when her gaze fell upon a dancer in the far corner. He was rather short and dressed in white flared trousers and high platform shoes. A huge pair of sunglasses hid most of his face. "Ooh," she said to Kirsty, pointing the dancer out. "*He's* a good dancer, isn't he?"

28

Kirsty looked at the boy. "Yes, he is," she agreed. "How strange that he's such a funky dancer, when everyone else is so terrible."

Rachel frowned thoughtfully. "Actually, the people who are dancing near him aren't that bad either," she said.

The girls stared at the boy as he whirled about the dance floor.

"I don't recognise him," Kirsty said after a moment or two. "I'm sure I haven't seen him at school before. I wonder if he's someone's little brother?"

Just then, the song finished and the girls edged forward, keen to get a better look at the dancing boy as he came to a stop.

Kirsty frowned as she spotted that he had unusually pointy ears, and even though the flashing disco lights were making everyone's faces turn funny colours, she was sure she could see a greenish tinge to his skin...

"Rachel!" Kirsty gulped. "I think that boy is really a *goblin*! Look at his ears!"

Rachel peered across the dance floor. "You're right!" she exclaimed. "He

must be the goblin with the Disco
Ribbon! *That's* why he's such
a good dancer."

Kirsty nodded, her eyes fixed on the
goblin who was now
dancing to the next
song, wiggling to
the beat on his
gigantic platform
shoes. "And that's
why everyone near
him is dancing well,"
she added. "The Disco

Ribbon's magic is affecting them, too!"

"Let's try and get closer," Rachel
suggested, "and see if we can spot the
magic ribbon."

Kirsty agreed. "Yes," she said. "We
might even be able to grab it without

him noticing, once we know where
it is. He's totally wrapped up in
the music."

The girls made their way across the
dance floor, dodging the
rather erratic dancing
that was going on
around them.
Things weren't
made any easier
by the fact that
there was now
quite a crowd
around the goblin, all
trying to copy his disco moves.

"I thought Jack Frost told his goblins
that they had to stay *hidden* with the
ribbons," Kirsty said to Rachel over the
thump of the music.

"He certainly isn't hiding," Rachel laughed. "But he is in disguise," she added, swerving to avoid a boy who had just managed to trip over his own feet. "Ow!" she gasped suddenly, as somebody else barged right into her, knocking her to the floor.

Kirsty bent down to help her friend up. It was only when the girls were both standing again that they realised something terrible had happened: the goblin had vanished!

# Goblin Goes Missing

"Oh, no!" said Rachel, looking around frantically. "Where is he?"

"I can't see him anywhere," Kirsty replied, "but look, the people who were near him are dancing badly now, just like everyone else. He must have gone."

Rachel, who was still staring around, suddenly spotted something rather strange. "Hey," she said. "Look at that glitter ball up there, Kirsty. Is it my imagination or is it shimmering more brightly than the others?"

She and Kirsty gazed up at the glitter ball – and then jumped with surprise as a tiny fairy darted out from behind it in a cloud of green sparkles.

"It's Jade the Disco Fairy!" Kirsty cried. "Thank goodness!"

The girls shielded their eyes from the bright lights as Jade waved at them, and then fluttered down to land on Kirsty's shoulder. Luckily, everyone else was so busy dancing badly and bumping into one another that they didn't notice a tiny fairy joining the disco!

Jade had long blonde hair. She wore a jade-green, halter-neck top, and trousers with a green, swirly print on them. On her feet she wore pretty, high-heeled green sandals.

"Hello, Jade," Rachel said as they moved to the side of the dance floor where it was a little quieter. "Did you see the goblin?"

"I certainly did," Jade said, rolling her eyes. "And I've never seen such a terrible outfit! It's enough to give disco a bad name! Those shoes – I mean, really!"

Kirsty laughed. "Did you see where he went?" she asked. "We lost him."

Jade shook her head. "I lost track of him too," she replied, "but he won't have gone far. If he's got my ribbon, I can guarantee that all he'll want to do is dance! He's bound to stay near the music."

"Well, he's not in the hall any more," Rachel said. "But maybe he's close by."

"Let's go out into the corridor," Kirsty suggested, walking towards a door nearby. "We can start looking there."

The girls and Jade went out of the hall. It was cooler and quieter in the corridor, although they could still hear the music from the disco quite clearly. They hurried along the corridor, peeping into the classrooms they passed.

The first two rooms were empty, but
as Kirsty popped her head around the
door of the third, she smiled to see the
goblin dancing on top of the desks and
singing really badly to the disco music.

She drew her head back quickly
before he spotted her. "He's in there!"
she hissed to Rachel and Jade. "What
shall we do?"

"Do?" Jade replied. "We'll go straight
in there and ask for my ribbon back,
that's what we'll do! Come on!"

# Ribbon In Reach

Jade zipped into the classroom, with Rachel and Kirsty right behind her. The goblin was now dancing away on a desk, which lay directly under a solar system mobile that dangled from the ceiling. He was having a great time, boogieing along to the music, his big high shoes banging loudly on the desk top with every step.

Jade fluttered over to him, and the girls gathered by his desk.

"I believe you've got my Disco Ribbon," Jade said. "And I'd like it back now, thank you very much!"

At her words, the goblin pushed his huge sunglasses off his face and almost fell off the desk in surprise to see Jade, Kirsty and Rachel in front of him.

"Go away! Can't you see I'm dancing?" he asked rudely, flicking his sunglasses down onto his nose again, and turning his back on the three friends.

Rachel watched him strutting his stuff. "I hate to say this, but he's actually quite good," she said in a low voice.

"I can't believe he can dance like that in those huge platforms!" Kirsty agreed.

Jade didn't look so impressed. "Hmmmph!" she sniffed crossly. "It's nothing to do with him. It's my ribbon's magic that's making him dance well, that's all."

The goblin danced around, clapping his hands in time to the music and wiggling his bottom.

45

As he came around to face the girls
again, he looked annoyed to see that
they were still there. Then a sly smirk
appeared on his face. "Hey, why don't
you come and join me?" he suggested.
"I could teach you my disco routine!"

Kirsty and Rachel shook their heads,
backing away warily.

"No chance," Rachel
replied. "We know
you just want to
freeze us!"
"And we're not
going to fall for
any of your tricks,"
Kirsty told him.

The goblin gave a cackle. "Well,
you're not getting this ribbon back!" he
said, pulling a length of sparkly green

out of his pocket.
"Maybe I'll freeze
you anyway, just
for the fun of it!"

He made a leap
towards the girls,
but Jade quickly
waved her wand and
turned them into fairies,
so that they could zoom out of his way.

Kirsty grinned as she flapped her
delicate wings and fluttered out of the
goblin's reach. Being able to fly was
such fun – and very useful!

The three fairies circled the goblin's
head as he glared at them. "Push off!"
he growled, climbing back on to his
table. "Can't a goblin dance in peace
if he wants to?"

"Not with my ribbon, he can't," Jade retorted. "Now hand it over, or we'll buzz around your head like annoying mosquitoes until you do!"

"Then I'll have to *swat* you like mosquitoes!" snarled the goblin, making another leap for them. He held his big hands flat like fly-swatters, and as he did so, the sparkly green Disco Ribbon flew out from between his fingers and looped around the model of Saturn on the solar system mobile above his head.

The goblin looked up and tugged at it, but the ribbon had got caught in Saturn's rings and wouldn't budge. "Stupid thing!" the goblin moaned, jumping up and down and yanking at it with all his might.

The solar system mobile swung dizzily, but the ribbon held fast.

Jade's eyes lit up. "This could be a chance to get my ribbon back!" she said to Rachel and Kirsty in a low voice. "How can we get the goblin to let go of the other end?"

Kirsty grinned. "Tickle him!" she suggested. She and Rachel had discovered on previous fairy adventures that the goblins were *extremely* ticklish.

Jade chuckled. "That's a brilliant idea," she said. "I'll tickle the goblin with my wand, and maybe you two could fly to the mobile and untangle the ribbon while he's distracted."

"Let's do it!" Rachel said eagerly.
Jade murmured some magic
words and her wand
suddenly grew much
longer and sprouted
a super-tickly, feathery
tip! "There," she
said with a smile.
"Let's see if this
does the trick."
She flew down
towards the goblin
and dusted the
feathery wand
under his arm while he
was reaching up to
pull on the ribbon.
He immediately shrieked
with laughter and lowered his

arm. "Ooh! Ooh! Stop it!" he yelped, still holding onto the ribbon and making the planets on the mobile clash together above his head.

Jade didn't stop. She wiggled the wand under his chin next, and the goblin collapsed in giggles.

"Ooh, no! No!" he chortled. "Stop!"

But the little fairy was a blur, flying all around the goblin, tickling him at the backs of his knees and behind his big ears until he was helpless with laughter. The girls watched as the goblin's grip on the ribbon began to slip.

Kirsty and Rachel flew up to the mobile and began trying to untangle the ribbon from Saturn's rings. By now, the goblin was laughing uncontrollably and his sunglasses flew off because his whole body was shaking with giggles. The goblin dropped to his knees, squirming and laughing, and then, to the girls' delight, he dropped the end of the Disco Ribbon.

# Bowled Over

"It worked!" Kirsty hissed excitedly, gazing at the dangling ribbon. "Quick, Rachel, we just have to untie this end and we'll have got it!"

"There!" Rachel cried, as the tangled end of the ribbon came free. She reached out to grab it, but before she could get a proper grip, the ribbon

slipped straight through her fingers and
fell onto the goblin's head!

"Oh, no!" Rachel cried, swooping
down to try and retrieve the ribbon.

The goblin, feeling the soft ribbon
land on his head, was so surprised that
he stopped laughing. Then he realised
what had happened and reached up to
grab the ribbon. With a look of
jubilation on his face, he stuffed it into

his trouser pocket and
jumped down from
the desk. "Can't
catch me!"
he yelled, and
then, sticking
his tongue out
rudely at the
three girls,

he ran straight out of the classroom.

Jade shook her wand, turning it back to normal at once. "After him!" she cried.

Jade, Kirsty and Rachel flapped their wings hard, zoomed across the classroom and soared back into the corridor, after the goblin.

The goblin seemed to be finding it hard to run on his platform shoes, Kirsty noticed. He was very wobbly, and stumbled a few times, although he still managed to keep ahead of the girls.

"Why is he so wobbly on his feet?"

Kirsty asked Jade. "I thought the ribbon helped him keep his balance even with those massive shoes."

"It does," Jade replied, "Just as long as he's disco dancing." She grinned. "But now that he's running instead of dancing, the ribbon's magic doesn't help."

Rachel, Kirsty and Jade flapped their wings even harder, but they

didn't seem able to gain on the goblin.

"We mustn't let him get away!"
Rachel cried.

The goblin ran past a door that led
into the disco hall, and the three fairies
raced after him. As they passed the
open door, Kirsty's eye was caught by
one of the sparkly glitter balls hanging
from the ceiling inside – and then
a brilliant idea popped into her head!

"Jade," she called quickly, "do you think you could conjure up a big glitter ball like the ones in the hall?"

Jade frowned. "Yes, of course," she said. "But why?"

"There's no time to explain," Kirsty said, "but could you just magic one up, please, and turn Rachel and me back into girls, too?"

"Sure," Jade replied, looking puzzled. She stopped flying and waved her wand  over Kirsty and Rachel. With a flurry of green sparkles, the girls' wings disappeared from their backs, and they were normal girls again.

Jade waved her wand a second time and a stream of green fairy dust swirled from its tip towards Kirsty. Instantly a sparkly green glitter ball appeared in Kirsty's arms.

"He's getting away!" Rachel called urgently, as the goblin got nearer to the end of the corridor.

"Yes, but not for long if you can bowl another strike!" Kirsty said, shoving the glitter ball into Rachel's hands. "Go on, Rachel! Bowl that goblin over!"

## Disco Divas

Rachel laughed as she realised what Kirsty had in mind. "I'll do my best," she said, bending down. Her eye firmly fixed on the running goblin, she took careful aim and bowled the glitter ball.

*Whoosh!* Along the corridor it rolled, perfectly straight, heading directly for the goblin. *CRASH!* It whacked right into the goblin's platform shoes, sending him flying!

"STRIKE!" Rachel, Kirsty and Jade cheered in the same breath, hurrying down the corridor to where the goblin lay sprawled on the floor.

"Great bowling, Rachel!" Jade declared.

"Thanks," Rachel said, with a grin. "Now where's the Disco Ribbon?"

As the girls arrived, the goblin was desperately trying to get to his feet. But he couldn't quite regain his balance and his arms flailed wildly as he tried to stand up on his huge platform shoes.

*Thump!* Down he went again, and, this time, the ribbon spilled out of his pocket. Kirsty quickly darted forward and snatched it  up before the goblin could even *think* about using freezing magic on her.

"Thanks Mr Goblin," she said, dodging smartly out of the goblin's way.

The goblin kicked off his platform shoes in a rage and got to his feet, rubbing his bottom where he'd bumped down on it and glowering at the girls.

"Stupid shoes! I'd have got away if it hadn't been for *them*!" he complained, and then he stomped off without another word, his big green feet slapping along the floor.

"Here you are, Jade," Kirsty said proudly, holding the Disco Ribbon up for the little fairy.

Jade waved her wand and green sparkles swirled all over the ribbon, making it shrink back to its Fairyland size.

"Thank you, girls," Jade said, smiling as she reattached the ribbon to the end

of her wand. A burst of sparkles surrounded the wand and the ribbon as they came together, and the ribbon seemed to glow an even deeper green. "That's more like it," Jade said, twirling her wand with a smile on her face. "Disco divas everywhere will move and groove a whole lot better now!"

"Great," Rachel said, beaming. "No more treading on toes at the school disco, then, I hope!"

Jade shook her head. "Definitely not," she replied. "Go and have a look, you'll see that everyone is having a much better time in the hall now."

"Hurrah!" Kirsty said, and then she strained to listen as a new song started up in the disco. "Oh, I love this one!" she exclaimed, doing a little dance on the spot. "Even the music seems better now, Jade!"

Jade grinned and kissed both girls. "Thanks again," she said. "Now go and have some fun. I can see Kirsty's dying to be a disco diva herself!"

"I'll do my best," Kirsty laughed. "Bye, Jade!"

"Bye," Rachel added, waving at the fairy. "Come on, Kirsty, let's hit the dance floor!"

Jade fluttered away down the corridor, leaving a trail of green sparkles in her wake, and Kirsty and Rachel boogied their way back into the school hall. Sure enough, the dance floor was full, and everyone was having fun. But, best of all, nobody was falling over or bumping into each other any more.

The two friends made their way onto the packed dance floor and joined in the dancing.

"I'm so glad we helped find the Disco Ribbon," Rachel called over to Kirsty with a grin. "This is brilliant fun!"

Kirsty nodded. "I know," she replied. Then she looked up and saw that there was a new glitter ball hanging from the ceiling – an extra-sparkly, *green* glitter

ball that sent thousands of jade
green lights whirling around the hall
as it spun.

"I love helping the fairies," Kirsty said
to Rachel, pointing out the glitter ball
with a grin. "And I can't wait to find
another one of the Dance Ribbons!"

**Now Rachel and Kirsty
must help...**

Rebecca the Rock 'n' Roll Fairy!

**Read on for a sneak peek...**

"Are you ready yet, Mum?" Kirsty
Tate called up the stairs. "Rachel and
I are dying to see your costumes!" She
grinned over at her best friend, Rachel
Walker, who was standing next to her.

"We'll be down soon," Mrs Tate called
back from the bedroom.

Kirsty and Rachel sat down on the
bottom stair to wait.

"I *wish* we were going to the rock 'n'
roll party with Mum and Dad," Kirsty
sighed. "It sounds like fun, *and* we might
find Rebecca the Rock 'n' Roll Fairy's

magic ribbon there!"

Rachel nodded. "The Dance Fairies are depending on us!" she reminded Kirsty.

Rachel and Kirsty had become friends with the fairies when they were holidaying on Rainspell Island, and now the girls were always eager to help whenever the fairies had a problem.

The main cause of trouble in Fairyland was mean Jack Frost, helped by his naughty goblin servants. A few days earlier, Jack Frost had asked the Dance Fairies to visit his ice castle and teach his goblins how to dance. But it was all a trick, so that the goblins could steal the Dance Fairies' magic ribbons!

When the King and Queen of Fairyland had demanded that the ribbons be given back, Jack Frost had refused. Instead he'd sent seven of his goblins tumbling into the human world, each clutching one of the ribbons. Now, during their half-term holiday, Kirsty and Rachel were helping the Dance Fairies to find their ribbons.

"We've made a good start," Kirsty remarked. "We've already found Bethany the Ballet Fairy's ribbon, and Jade the Disco Fairy's too."

"But if we don't find the rest, all the other kinds of dancing will keep on going wrong, and dancing won't be fun any more!" Rachel sighed...

Read Rebecca the Rock 'n' Roll Fairy
to find out what adventures are in store for Kirsty and Rachel!

# Meet the
# Dance Fairies

Jack Frost has stolen the Dance Fairies' magic ribbons! Kirsty and Rachel must get them back, or dance everywhere will be ruined.

# www.rainbowmagicbooks.co.uk

# RAINBOW magic®

Meet the fairies, play games
and get sneak peeks at
the latest books!

There's fairy fun for everyone at

## www.rainbowmagicbooks.co.uk

You'll find great activities, competitions, stories and
fairy profiles, and also a special newsletter.

# Win Rainbow Magic Goodies!

There are lots of Rainbow Magic fairies, and we want to know
which one is your favourite! Send us a picture of her and tell
us in thirty words why she is your favourite and why you like
Rainbow Magic books. Each month we will put the entries into
a draw and select one winner to receive a Rainbow Magic
Sparkly T-shirt and Goody Bag!

Send your entry on a postcard to Rainbow Magic Competition,
Orchard Books, 338 Euston Road, London NW1 3BH.
Australian readers should email: childrens.books@hachette.com.au
New Zealand readers should write to Rainbow Magic Competition,
PO Box 3255, Shortland St, Auckland 1140, NZ.
Don't forget to include your name and address.
Only one entry per child.

# Good luck!

# Meet the
# Sporty Fairies

Join Rachel and Kirsty as they help the Sporty Fairies
to foil Jack Frost's naughty plot to mess up
the Fairyland Olympics!

## www.rainbowmagicbooks.co.uk